Ten Naughty Little Monkeys

By **Suzanne Williams**
Illustrated by **Suzanne Watts**

HarperCollinsPublishers

Library of Congress Cataloging-in-Publication Data is available.
ISBN-10: 0-06-059904-9 — ISBN-13: 978-0-06-059904-1
ISBN-10: 0-06-059905-7 (lib. bdg.) — ISBN-13: 978-0-06-059905-8 (lib. bdg.)

Typography by Rachel L. Schoenberg
2 3 4 5 6 7 8 9 10
❖
First Edition

For Ward and Emily, whose monkeyshines
continue to amaze and delight me
—S. Williams

For little Sophia, with love from Mummy
—S. Watts

TEN little monkeys
Jumping on the bed.

One fell off
And bumped her head.

Mama called the doctor,
And the doctor said,

"No more monkeys
Jumping on the bed."

NINE little monkeys
Racing out the door.
One monkey tripped
And landed on the floor.

Mama called the doctor,
And the doctor roared,
"No more monkeys
Racing out the door!"

EIGHT little monkeys
Skating in the street.
One monkey slipped
And plopped on her seat.

Mama called the doctor.
He didn't miss a beat.
"No more monkeys
Skating in the street."

SEVEN little monkeys
Climbing up a tree.

One tumbled out
And skinned his knee.

Mama called the doctor.
He said, "Can we agree?
No more monkeys
Climbing up a tree."

SIX little monkeys
Rolling down a hill.
One hit a bump
And took a big spill.

Mama called the doctor.
The doctor sounded ill.
"No more monkeys
Rolling down a hill."

FIVE little monkeys
Hiking down the trail.
One monkey flipped
And bent his tail.

Mama called the doctor,
And the doctor wailed,
"No more monkeys
Hiking down the trail!"

FOUR little monkeys
Fishing off the dock.

One toppled in,
To everybody's shock.

Mama called the doctor,
And the doctor squawked,
"No more monkeys
Fishing off the dock!"

THREE little monkeys
Playing hide-and-seek.
One tipped over
And started to shriek.

Mama called the doctor.
He almost couldn't speak.
"No more monkeys
Playing hide-and-seek!"

TWO little monkeys,
Dressing up in clothes,
Tripped wearing heels
And stubbed their toes.

Mama called the doctor.
Now what do you suppose?
"No more monkeys
Dressing up in clothes!"

ONE little monkey
Following a map
Didn't see the net
And fell into a trap.

Mama called the doctor,
And the doctor snapped,
"Put those monkeys
Down for a nap!"

TEN little monkeys
Jumping on the bed.